THE AMAZING WORLD OF

STUART

SARA PENNYPACKER
With illustrations by MARTIN MATJE

Scholastic Inc.
New York Toronto London Auckland
Sydney Mexico City New Delhi Hong Kong

No part of this publication may be reproduced, stored in a retrieval system, or transmitted in any form or by any means, electronic, mechanical, photocopying, recording, or otherwise, without written permission of the publisher. For information regarding permission, write to Scholastic Inc., Attention: Permissions Department, 557 Broadway, New York, NY 10012.

Library of Congress Cataloging-in-Publication Data is available.

Stuart's Cape, ISBN 978-0-439-30180-0
Text copyright © 2002 by Sara Pennypacker
Illustrations copyright © 2002 by Martin Matje

Stuart Goes to School, ISBN 978-0-439-30182-4
Text copyright © 2003 by Sara Pennypacker
Illustrations copyright © 2003 by Martin Matje

Stuart's Cape was originally published in hardcover by Orchard Books in 2002. *Stuart Goes to School* was originally published in hardcover by Orchard Books in 2003.

ISBN 978-0-545-17842-6

12 11 10 9 8 7 6 5 4 3 2 1   10 11 12 13 14 15/0

Printed in the U.S.A.   40

First compilation printing, July 2010

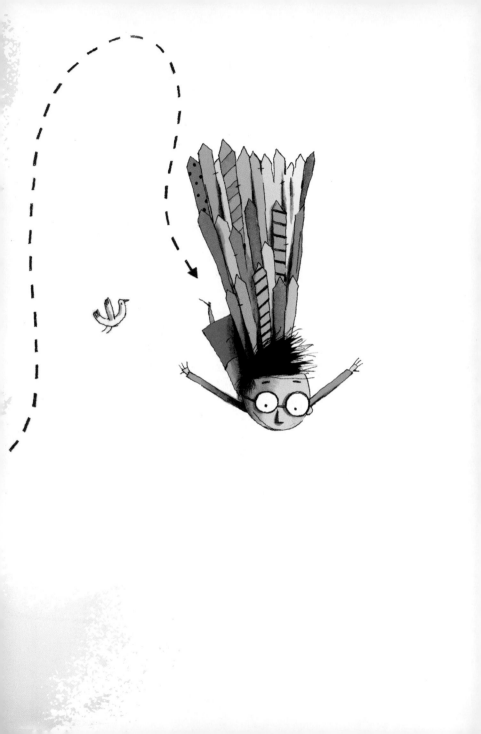

Sara
Pennypacker

STUART'S CAPE

Illustrated by
Martin Matje

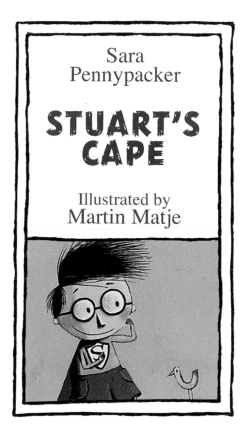

For Stuart, of course.
S.P.

To my mother, who gave me my cape.
M.M.

STUART MAKES A CAPE

"I want to have an adventure," Stuart moaned for the third time. He mushed his face against the rainy window and squinted. This made the world look smeary. It was fun, but not fun enough.

"I don't have anyone to play with. I can't build anything because all my stuff is gone. I've played horses and dinosaurs and gorillas all morning. Now I want to do something different."

"School starts in a few days," his mother reminded him. "That will be something different."

Stuart had not forgotten this. He had been worrying all week.

Stuart and his family had just moved to Punbury, so he had a lot to worry about. What if there were man-eating spiders in his new bedroom closet? Or, a man eating spiders? What if he got lost? Worst of all, he would be in a new school for third grade. Hundreds of things could go wrong. What if he couldn't find the bathroom? What if he *could* find the bathroom, but he got

WORRY

locked inside? What if no one wanted to be his friend?

Stuart was very good at worrying. He was not so good at waiting.

"Anyway," he sighed, "in a few days is *in a few days*. I want an adventure *now*." He slid down to the floor, next to his cat, to think.

"I wish I were Whizzer the Space Boy," he said to One-Tooth. "I would put on my cape and save a planet. I wish I were Power

Tool Man, or Rubberlegs Roger. I would put on my cape and . . ."

Stuart smacked his head and jumped up. *"Of course!"* he shouted. "Adventures only happen to people with *capes!*"

"Nonsense," said his mother. "People can have adventures in dresses, or nice, warm sweaters."

"In business suits or pajamas," added his father.

"Nope," said Stuart, shaking his head. "The cape is the thing. It must be a rule. I can't even think of one person who ever had an adventure without one. Can you?"

Stuart's mother scrunched her eyes down, thinking hard. His father scratched his chin, thinking hard. Aunt Bubbles tugged her braids, thinking hard. Three lemons fell out. "Oh, good!" she cried. "I was wondering where I packed those."

Aunt Bubbles went into the kitchen to make lemonade. Stuart's parents followed her to make sure nothing exploded. One-Tooth followed them all to see if tuna fish were involved.

Stuart, Stuart said to himself, *you need a cape.*

The hall was full of boxes from moving. None of them was his, though.

Stuart had packed up his best stuff and left it outside for the moving van. But the trash collector had taken it instead! His extremely valuable things, mistaken for trash! A mannequin arm, an oven door, a dead Christmas tree. A cracked toilet seat, a box of bent coat hangers, false teeth . . .

STUFF
FROM
UNCLE
NESTOR'S
MAGIC ACT

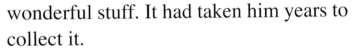

wonderful stuff. It had taken him years to collect it.

Stuart poked around in the boxes. No capes. Just some junk his family was throwing out.

A bunch of old ties. A rusty stapler. One purple sock.

"Hmmm . . ." said Stuart.

One by one, side by side, very carefully, Stuart stapled the ties together. One hundred ties made a wonderful cape! Heavy and smooth and long. Inside, he stapled the purple sock for a secret pocket.

Stuart put the cape on. Things felt different right away.

Very different.

Stuart ran to the hall mirror. He threw his shoulders back and puffed up his chest. He stretched his mouth wide, but not in a smile. He twisted around so he was looking (boldly) over one shoulder. In this position it was hard to see himself in the mirror. He had to slide his eyeballs around to the edges of his eyes. But it was worth it.

Because there in the mirror was someone who was sure to have adventures. There in the mirror was —

Just then the doorbell rang.

Well, he would think up a name later.

PLAYING STUART

S tuart ran to answer the doorbell. On the doorstep stood a dinosaur, a horse, and a gorilla. Dripping wet.

"Hello," said Stuart, in his most normal voice. "Come on in."

He knew one thing about people who wore capes: They never acted surprised. Even if they went zinging around the solar system, like Whizzer the Space Boy. Even if their arms turned into drills, like Power

Tool Man. Even if they could bounce over parking lots, like Rubberlegs Roger. From now on, no matter what happened, Stuart would not act surprised.

One-Tooth did not care about not acting surprised. Her eyes bulged out like Ping-Pong balls. Her fur stood up like flames. She tore up the curtains and glared down at the animals.

The visitors did not look happy, either.

"You have been playing animals again. And you do it all wrong," said the dinosaur. "All that crashing around."

"All that trotting and jumping," added the horse.

"All that swinging from branches," grumbled the gorilla. "It's ridiculous. We don't do those things at all."

"What do you do?" asked Stuart, greatly interested.

"Well, we eat," said the gorilla.

"Yes, we eat," said the horse. "And we stand."

"We eat and we stand," said the dinosaur. "And we sleep!" He leaned back into the sofa. "It's very hard to get it right."

"Besides," snorted the horse, "it's rude. We don't pretend to be you."

"You could," Stuart said. "You could play Stuart. I wouldn't mind."

The animals looked at each other. "How would we play it? What do you do?"

"Follow me." Stuart led the animals to his bedroom. "First, I wake up."

"Let me try," said the dinosaur. He jumped onto Stuart's bed.

"I, Stuart, am awake!" cried the dinosaur. "This is a good game so far."

CRASH!!

"Stuart!" called his mother from the kitchen. "Are you jumping on your bed again?"

"Of course not!" Stuart called back.

He pointed to his closet. "I get dressed next. I have to watch out for man-eating spiders."

The horse went in and stomped around for a while. He came out sort-of dressed. "Do I look like you?" he asked.

"Sometimes," said Stuart.

"Stuart!" cried Aunt Bubbles. "Are you stomping around in your closet again?"

"I wasn't even *in* my closet!" Stuart answered.

He showed the animals the bathroom. "Next, I get cleaned up."

The gorilla got the idea right away. He turned on the water. He unrolled the toilet paper and squirted toothpaste

all over the floor. "Like this?" he asked.

"Yep," said Stuart. "Exactly."

"Stuart!" yelled his father. "Are you playing in the bathroom again?"

"Oh, no," Stuart yelled back. "Not me!"

"Playing Stuart gets pretty hard now," he told the animals, going back into the living room. "Every day I have to figure out what to do. School starts soon. When there's no school, I like to play with my friends. Except I haven't made any. Or I build things. Except all my stuff is gone."

Stuart heaved a deep sigh of sadness. "Anyway, it's raining today."

"And you eat when it's raining?" asked the horse hopefully.

"I play inside. Games like . . ." Stuart paused to think of an easy one. "Hide-and-seek! I'll teach you. You all hide, and I'll close my eyes. Then I'll find you."

The animals scrambled to hide.

"Stuart!" shouted his family. "What is going on? It sounds like a herd of wild animals in there!"

"Don't worry!" Stuart answered. "There are only three animals here. And they're not *too* wild."

The animals had not hidden very well. But it was their first time, so Stuart pretended he could not find them.

Just then his family came running out of the kitchen. "What do you mean, *three animals*?" they cried. "We don't see any animals!"

"Of course not," said Stuart. He winked. "They are hiding."

"Oh." Stuart's family winked back. "We understand."

"They came over because of my cape," Stuart explained. "It's magic."

"Of *course* it is." Stuart's family smiled. "And now we are going to pay some magic bills."

"It was fun playing Stuart," said the

animals when Stuart found them. "But not as much fun as eating. What have you got to eat?"

Aunt Bubbles worked in a bakery. Every day she brought home the leftovers. Stuart found apple pie and bagels and chocolate chip cookies. The animals ate nearly everything in the house. Stuart himself was very hungry. He ate an entire angel food cake.

"Very good," said the animals. "Quite tasty." Then they wiped their mouths with their tails.

Stuart wiped the cake crumbs from his mouth with his new cape.

"Well, good night," said his new friends. "If you get bored again, you may play animals."

"Thanks," said Stuart. He looked down at his new cape and smiled. "But I don't think I'll be getting bored again."

STUART FLIES

Stuart woke up on the ceiling. "Good," he said, remembering not to act surprised. "I can fly."

He flapped his cape and zoomed around his bedroom, getting the hang of it. Then he flew into the kitchen.

"I can fly today!" he cried to his family. "I'm going to have an adventure every day now that I have a cape."

Stuart's father was watching TV. "Quiet!" he said. "It's time for the banking news."

Stuart's mother was reading the paper. "Hush!" she said. "There is a big sale at the E-Z Mart. One toothbrush for the price of two!"

Aunt Bubbles was coloring. "Shhhh!" she said. "I'm trying to draw cake. Eat your breakfast."

LOST

angel food cake
~~big~~ reward
HUGE

Stuart pulled himself down the refrigerator and along the counter. He grabbed the table. His legs floated in the air. "May I please have some tape?" he asked.

Aunt Bubbles didn't look up from her poster. She gave Stuart the tape. Stuart rolled it into big, sticky balls. He stuck them onto the back of his cape. Now he could sit.

"I guess my cape is magic," Stuart tried again. "I can fly."

"Don't be silly," said his mother. "People can't fly."

"That's impossible!" said his father. "People can't fly."

"It's very hard to draw cake!" said Aunt Bubbles. "Especially when people are talking! Now go outside and play."

"Okay," Stuart sighed. "But I don't think that's such a good idea."

Stuart peeled off the tape balls. Up he rose, like a balloon. He flew to the door.

"Good-bye!" he called.

"Good-bye!" his family called back. They never looked up. "Have a nice day!"

Of course, as soon as Stuart flew outside, he soared up. And up.

There was a lot to do. He bounced back and forth, pretending he was a tennis ball.

He flapped straight out, pretending he was a flag. He zigzagged across the sky, pretending he was a bolt of lightning. Stuart was so busy he forgot to feel lonely. He could do anything.

Except come down.

Some crows flew by.

"Good morning," Stuart said. "Fine day for flying."

And it was. The air was as soft and cool as whipped cream. Down below, the houses looked like chocolate chips in a little cookie town.

But it was a fine day for worrying, too.

Stuart looked down. What if all those little houses were full of robbers? What if there were wolves in his backyard, or enormous snakes? And what if no one ever wanted to be his friend?

Now Stuart had something else to worry about. How was he going to get down?

Aunt Bubbles came outside. "Where is

that boy?" she asked. "He should come in for lunch now." Her voice was very tiny.

"Up here!" Stuart shouted.

Aunt Bubbles looked all around. "My stars!" she screamed. "The clouds are talking!" She never thought the little speck in the sky was her nephew.

"All this excitement is making me hungry!" yelled Aunt Bubbles. "Too bad someone stole my angel food cake yesterday. It was lighter than air."

Yikes! Stuart thought. *It WAS lighter than air!*

"Run to the bakery! Get a pound cake!" he shouted. "A great big heavy one. Quick!"

Aunt Bubbles did. "Now what, clouds?"

"Cut the tires off the car," Stuart called down to her. "Tie them together to that split tree. Make a slingshot."

"I understand, clouds!" shouted Aunt Bubbles. She fit the cake into the big slingshot. She pulled it back.

The pound cake shot up like a rocket. Stuart flew over and caught it.

Slowly, bite by bite, Stuart came back down. He landed softly on the roof. He ate the last crumb as he floated down the chimney.

"Oh, there you are!" said Stuart's mother. "We had quite a day! Aunt Bubbles cut the tires off the car. She thought the clouds were hungry."

"Too bad you missed it," said his father.

"Your parents were right," said Aunt Bubbles. "People *can* have adventures without capes!"

Stuart just smiled.

STUART GROWS TOAST

S tuart wanted toast. There wasn't any.
"Oh, rats," he said. "Toast is my
favorite food."

He made a list.

Why I Like Toast:

1) Warm
2) You can put stuff on it
3) Stays where you put it
   because it is not slimy
4) Smells good
5) Fits in your pocket

In your pocket! Stuart remembered! He was wearing his new cape! He checked the secret pocket. No toast. What kind of a cape was this? But wait . . . three seeds!

Stuart smiled. "Of course," he said. "Toast seeds." *That's* the kind of cape it was.

Stuart went outside. He planted the seeds in a nice sunny spot.

"What are you doing?" asked his parents.

"Growing toast," answered Stuart.

"You can't grow toast," said his parents. "Now good-bye. We're going to buy new tires for the car."

"What are you doing?" asked Aunt Bubbles.

"Growing toast," answered Stuart.

"Good idea," said Aunt Bubbles. "I'll make tea."

Stuart watered the seeds with melted butter. "OK," he said. "Now grow."

And they did. Three nice, big plants

popped up at once. *Like toast from a toaster*, thought Stuart. At the tip of each plant was a little bundle of leaves.

Stuart peeled open the first green bundle. It was the size of his smallest fingernail. Inside was an even smaller piece of buttered toast!

Stuart tried to pluck it from the plant. But the tiny buttered toast was slippery. It slid out of his fingers and landed butter side down. It was ant food now.

But there were still two more plants.

And the bundles had grown! They were now the size of his hand! Stuart peeled open the second bundle.

Just then the mailman passed by. "My goodness!" he said. "What is that marvelous smell?"

"I grew toast," said Stuart. "Would you like some?"

Stuart picked the toast from the second plant. He gave it to the mailman.

"Delicious!" the mailman exclaimed. "That is the best toast I have ever tasted. Thank you so much! Now I must be on my way."

"You're welcome," said Stuart. "Goodbye."

Stuart turned to the third plant. The bundle had grown again! It was the size of his head!

How big could toast get? Stuart wondered.

The seeds had come from his new cape. Anything was possible.

Stuart squeezed his eyes shut. He waited and he waited.

While he waited, he worried. He had to go to school tomorrow. What if his number fives came out backward? What if he was the shortest kid in third grade? What if he didn't make a friend?

Worrying really was his best thing. Waiting really was his worst thing.

SCHOOL
TOMORROW
all
alone
NO
friend
SHORT
the
SHORTEST
in the third
grade

Stuart opened his eyes. It was hard not to act surprised.

The last bundle was ENORMOUS!

He climbed up on a stump to peel back the leaves.

The toast inside smelled heavenly. It was warm and crunchy and perfectly buttered. And it was the size of a car! Well, a pretty flat car.

"Aunt Bubbles!" Stuart called. "Help!"

Together they dragged the enormous toast inside and brushed the grass off.

Stuart got a saw and sawed off some strips. They were as big as fence posts. "This is a lot of toast," he said. "Call the neighbors. Tell them to come to a toast party."

Everyone brought something to put on the toast strips. There was jam and jelly, of course. There was applesauce and cheddar cheese. There was strawberry yogurt and peanut butter and hamburgers. Someone brought hot fudge. One-Tooth hogged the tuna fish, but everyone else was good about sharing.

Sadly, none of the neighbors was going into the third grade.

But on the bright side, none of them seemed to be robbers. And none of them had noticed any wolves or enormous snakes hanging around the neighborhood.

Everything was delicious, and the toast stayed warm. Finally, when no one could eat another bite, the party was over.

"Good night, good night," the neighbors called. "We had a wonderful time!"

There was still a huge piece of toast left.

"Where are we going to put this?" Aunt Bubbles asked. "It's as big as a mattress."

Stuart smiled. He pulled out his list and crossed off number five.

"These are all good things for a food

Why I Like Toast:

1) Warm
2) You can put stuff on it
3) Stays where you put it because it is not slimy
4) Smells good
5) File in your pocket

to be. But they are also good things for a bed to be."

Aunt Bubbles helped Stuart push the toast into his room. They pushed his old, broken-by-the-dinosaur bed out the window. They piled quilts and pillows on his new toast bed.

"Lots of quilts," Stuart said. "I don't want crumbs."

Stuart was almost asleep when his parents came home.

"Good night, son," they said. "Are you warm enough?"

"Oh sure," said Stuart. "Warm as toast."

A BAD START

Stuart woke up worried. School really started tomorrow, but today was orientation day. A note had come. New students could visit a day early for orientation if they wanted to. It was kind of a practice day.

"What a good idea!" Stuart's mother had exclaimed. "An extra first day. You can get used to things!"

What a terrible idea, Stuart had thought.

An extra first day. Twice as many things could go wrong.

What if he did something stupid, and the other kids pointed at him and laughed? What if they laughed so hard they fell down on the playground? Then he'd never make any friends. Not after making everyone fall down on the playground.

Stuart flopped back down. His toast bed made a nice crunchy sound, but he couldn't enjoy it.

He was eight years old, and his life was ruined.

Then he sat up again.

Wait a minute. He had a cape! He'd probably have a really great adventure right in the middle of school! And all the kids would want to be his friend!

Stuart ran downstairs, starving. He slid into the kitchen, and his cape flapped out just right.

"Whoa, there!" his parents said at exactly the same time. "You can't wear your cape to school."

"I have to wear it every day," Stuart reminded them, pulling a jar of strawberry

jam from the cupboard. "So adventures will happen. So the kids will want to be my friend."

Stuart's parents glared down at him with their no-argument looks.

Luckily, Stuart had been practicing his own no-argument look in the mirror.

This was a good time to try it out.

"Something in your eye?" asked his father, untying Stuart's cape.

"Do you have a stomachache?" asked his mother, folding it up.

Stuart grew weaker and weaker as he dragged himself across the kitchen to the table. He looked behind him to see if he was leaving a trail of melted bones.

His mother set his cape on the table. "There now, all ready for when you come home." One-Tooth curled up on the cape.

"Maybe that cape *is*

magic!" laughed his father. "That maniac cat of yours is taking a nap, even though it's trash collection day!"

Tipping over trash cans was One-Tooth's favorite thing to do. Usually Stuart thought this was extremely funny, but today he moaned. He remembered what had happened on trash collection day last week. All his best stuff, gone.

"Eat your breakfast, Stuart," his mother said.

"You don't want to be late," his father said.

Stuart collapsed into his chair. How could his parents sound so cheerful? Hundreds of things could go wrong today. It was bad enough he didn't have a friend. Now he had to face it all without his cape.

Stuart tried to lift his toast. "Not . . . strong . . . enough . . ." he murmured. Even his tongue felt weak, but he licked a little strawberry jam off his toast. It tasted sad, like red glue, and it stuck in his throat.

"Good-bye, good-bye!" Stuart's family sang out the door. "Have a nice day!"

Stuart's father was going off to his job as a carpet cleaner. His mother was going off to her job at the beauty shop. Aunt Bubbles was going off to her job at the bakery.

None of them seemed to notice how dangerously weak he was.

"Mmff-hhmm," Stuart replied. "Glaaaaahhhhkkkk."

He was off to become a total flop as a third grader.

TRADING PLACES

S tuart was so weak he could barely walk. At the end of his street, he sat down on the sidewalk to rest. He watched a tiny ant crawl down into a crack in the sidewalk.

How he wished he could trade places with that ant!

He would just shrink down and disappear into that little crack. He'd build tunnels and eat cracker crumbs. So what if he didn't have a friend? All he'd have to worry about would be not getting squished.

Of course, if he traded places with the ant, the ant would have to trade places with him. That's how trading places worked.

Stuart stretched out on the warm sidewalk to think about an ant going to orientation day.

A loud crash down the street ruined his daydream.

Stuart saw a garbage truck, he saw his cape, and he saw his cat.

"*Stop, One-Tooth!*" Stuart shouted.

One-Tooth's one tooth poked out of an enormous cat grin. She did not stop.

As One-Tooth backed up to ram into

another bunch of trash cans, Stuart leaped onto the truck. He waded through all the trash and climbed up to the driver's seat.

"Move over," Stuart said firmly. He took the cape off his cat. He put it around his own shoulders and took a deep breath of the good tie-and-magic smell. At this exact moment, he could feel all his strength rushing back to him. He knew what he had to do.

Luckily, driving was a lot easier than grown-ups pretended it was. One pedal to go, another to stop. Steer. But collecting the trash was a big job. Street after street, lined with trash cans. It took hours. At every stop, Stuart found something too good to throw away.

A curly wig, a box full of doorknobs, a bag of keys.

He put all these things up front with him. "Someone should do something with this great stuff," he said to his cat. "I wonder

where the trashman is."

One-Tooth didn't answer. She was sound asleep, making a funny rattling sound. Exactly like snoring.

But only people snored, not cats.

And then Stuart realized a terrible thing.

Of course! One-Tooth had traded places with the trashman! And if she had traded places with the trashman, then that meant . . .

Stuart turned the truck around and

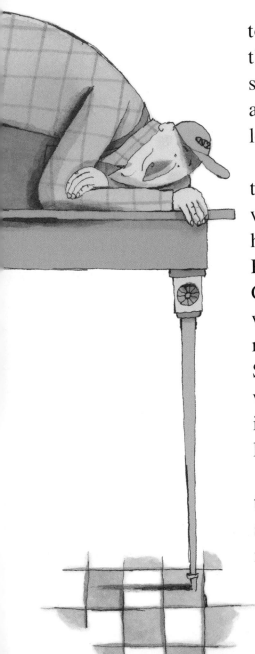

tore back down the street. He screeched to a stop at his house and leaped down.

Curled up on the kitchen table was a man. His hat said STANLEY, PUNBURY TRASH COLLECTOR, and he was making a funny rumbling sound. Stuart wished it were snoring. But it sounded an awful lot like purring.

Gently, so as not to startle him, Stuart shook the trashman's shoulder.

The trashman

yawned and stretched. He began to lick his wrist.

"Please don't do that!" Stuart cried.

The trashman blinked, and then rolled over onto his back.

Too late. Stanley, the Punbury trash collector, had turned into a cat.

Fleas. Hairballs. Raw mice for breakfast. And he, Stuart, was responsible for the mess. All because he had taken off his cape. He would spend the rest of his life in his room. Or in jail.

Unless he could change One-Tooth and Stanley back again.

Stuart grabbed a can of Kat Krunchees from the shelf, shook it, and headed outside. The trashman leaped off the table and followed, licking his

KAT
Krunchees

100%.Good

lips. He followed Stuart right up onto the seat of his truck.

Stuart lifted his cat to the ground. One-Tooth took off after a squirrel. The trashman stared at Stuart as though he had never seen him before. It had worked.

"You were sleeping," Stuart explained. "Having a little catnap. Do you feel okay now?"

"Fine," answered Stanley. "But I can't nap. I have to do my work."

"Don't worry," Stuart told him. "It's all done. I collected all the trash in the neighborhood."

"Well, thank you," answered the trashman, sadly. "But that's not my work. That's just my job."

"Then what is your work?" Stuart asked, confused.

"I'll show you," the trashman said, pointing to an enormous barn at the end of the street.

Stanley drove Stuart to the barn and threw open the big doors.

Stuart had never felt so excited in his whole life. He trembled all over. Even his eyes were shaking slightly, but he could still see.

Row after row of tables piled high with neat stacks of useful things. Faucets, broomsticks, and broken TVs. Picture frames, bathtubs, and bicycle wheels. A saddle, a screen door, a chair without legs.

"People throw great stuff away all the time. They think it's junk, just because it's old, or broken a little. Maybe they don't see how great it could be. Maybe they're too busy to fix it. Anyway, saving it is my

work. Too bad about today, now I'll never know what was out there. . . ."

"Wait!" Stuart shouted.

He showed the trashman all the great things he had saved.

"I can't believe it!" the trashman cried, wiping a tear from his eye. "Nobody else has ever understood. We can be partners in junk saving!"

Stuart and Stanley shook hands. They shared a snack of toast, and talked some more about trash. "Every day there's some new treasure in the trash," Stanley said. "And I never know what it will be. That's the best part."

"I know what you mean," Stuart answered. "It's like my cape. Every day something different happens. I never know what it will be. And that's the best part."

"Of course, saving junk is a big responsibility," Stanley said.

"My cape is a big responsibility, too,"

Stuart agreed. "I can't let anyone else wear it. I can never, ever, *ever* take it off."

Stuart knew he could explain this to his family. They liked the word *responsibility*. They used it a lot. He would always wear his cape, even when he went to —

"Yikes!" Stuart cried, jumping up. "School!"

Stanley gave him a ride to Punbury Elementary School, and Stuart raced inside to room 3B. No one was there except the teacher.

"Sorry I'm late!" he said. "The trashman turned into a cat, and I had to collect all the trash. But don't worry, I'm never going to take off my cape again!"

Mrs. Spindles stared at Stuart. "I think this is going to be an interesting year. But I'm sorry you didn't get to meet the other students. Maybe you could have made a friend."

Stuart smiled. That was exactly what he had just done.

THE
END

STUART'S advice column

Don't leave anything good outside on trash collection day.

If you're sharing food with a ~~dinosor~~ dinosaur, take some for yourself FIRST.

There are no bathrooms in the sky.

Tuna fish and grape jelly don't taste good together (even on toast).

Try out your no-argument look on a little kid <u>FIRST</u>!

Sara
Pennypacker

STUART
GOES TO
SCHOOL

Illustrated by
Martin Matje

BAD
DAY

DAY
1

DAY ONE

As soon as he woke up, Stuart knew it was going to be a bad day. You can smell a bad day coming. It smells a lot like sour milk.

The first bad thing about the day was hanging on his bedpost. A pair of green plaid pants, so bright they hurt his eyes. A shirt with little cowboys on it.

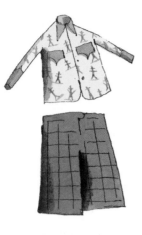

First day
of school
suit

Stuart was excellent at worrying. In fact, worrying was his best thing. But he had forgotten to worry about this. Every year, his mother made him dress up for the first day of school. In clothes nobody else would wear.

Stuart and his family had just moved to Punbury. He would be new at school, so he already had plenty to worry about. What if he forgot everything he learned in second grade? What if he couldn't find the bathroom? What if he *could* find the bathroom, but he got stuck inside and the teacher had to get him out with *firemen?* What if nobody wanted to be his friend?

And now this: green plaid hurt-your-eyes pants and a cowboy shirt. Where did his mother even *find* clothes like these?

"Stuart," he heard his mother call. "I left you a nice new outfit. It was your father's when he was in third grade! Now isn't *that* something?"

Stuart buried himself under his quilt. It would be impossible to make friends now. The other kids were going to fall down left and right laughing at him. Even cowboys would fall down left and right laughing at him.

He poked his head back out.
Wait a minute. He had a cape now. He had made it last week out of a hundred old ties. Just as he'd hoped, magical things had been happening since he had started wearing it. Adventures. A different one each day.

So far, the magical thing of the day had been a surprise. But *maybe . . .*

Stuart pointed his brain at the ugly outfit. He squeezed his eyes shut and concentrated powerful brain waves on making it *disappear*. He concentrated hard until he smelled brain-smoke coming from behind his eyeballs. He opened his eyes.

The outfit was still there. It looked more horrible than before.

Stuart sighed deeply and got out of bed. He put on the awful clothes and wrapped his cape around himself. One good thing about a cape: At least no one could see what he was wearing underneath. He could go to school in his underwear if he wanted to.

Not that he wanted to, of course.

Stuart's family was eating breakfast when he came downstairs.

"Good morning," said his father cheerfully. He was going off to his job as a carpet cleaner.

"Good morning," said his mother cheerfully. She was going off to her job as a beautician.

"Good morning," said Aunt Bubbles cheerfully. She was going off to her job as a baker.

VERY
BAD
DAY

"I don't think it's a good morning," answered Stuart glumly. He was going off to be a total flop as a third grader.

Stuart had a lot to worry about, so he spread it out.

On the bus ride he worried about the bathroom thing, of course. And what if he were the shortest kid in the class?

Climbing up the big steps to school, he worried that his fives might come out backward while he was at the blackboard. And what if someone brought egg salad for

lunch, and the smell made him throw up?

Dragging himself down the long hall to room 3B he worried about getting locked inside his locker. And what if a wasp were hiding inside his juice carton at snack time and stung him, and his lip swelled up like a water balloon?

Stuart found the seat with his name tag and began worrying about the bathroom thing again. If worrying were a sport, he would have a neck full of gold medals by now.

"Good morning, children," said the teacher. "My name is Mrs. Spindles. Would anyone like to start by sharing something for Our Big Interesting World?"

A girl in the front row bounced up and down in her seat so hard that a bunch of barrettes went flying. But she had about a hundred left in her hair.

"Yes, Olivia?" Mrs. Spindles called on her.

"My daddy went away on important business last week. He brought me back this pocketbook. It has real plastic diamonds on it."

"This used to be a muffin," said a boy named Nacho, proudly holding up a green lump. "I saved it under my bed all summer!"

Everyone in the class said, *"Cool, Nacho,"* except for Olivia, who was still looking for her barrettes.

Stuart smacked his head and groaned. Our Big Interesting World was the third grade name for show-and-tell. He wished he had something interesting to show. Like the false teeth he had found in the trash yesterday. Or the squashed toad from his driveway. Then all the kids would say, *"Cool, Stuart."*

But wait! He did have something to show! Something so great that all the kids would fight over who could be his friend.

Stuart's hand shot up. He jumped around in his seat. If he'd been wearing barrettes they would have gone flying into the next classroom.

"Yes, Stuart?" Mrs. Spindles said. "Do you have something interesting to show us?"

"*Yesss!*" shouted Stuart as he ran to the front of the room. This was going to be great!

"I made this cape!" Stuart told the class. "I stapled a hundred ties together, and it's magic! Every day I have a new adventure. And look! I put a secret purple pocket inside."

Stuart whipped open his cape very dramatically. He had practiced this in front of the mirror a lot.

He waited for the kids to say, "*Awesome!*" or "*Wow!*" or "*Cool, Stuart!*"

He waited for a long time. The room was so silent Stuart wondered if his ears had stopped working.

He felt an odd breeze. He looked down and froze in horror.

The awful new outfit had disappeared, just as he had wished. But now he was wearing nothing but his underpants. In front of the entire class!

He snapped his cape shut, but it was too late. All the kids began to laugh. When Stuart was embarrassed, his ears got embarrassed. As the kids laughed, he could feel his ears begin to blow up, like sausages on a grill. Bigger and redder and hotter they grew, until suddenly the room went quiet again.

"Wow!" said Olivia. "Exactly the color of my Malibu Sunset Fashion barrettes."

"Wow!" said Nacho, holding two pieces of red construction paper up to his head. "Giant mutant alien radar ears."

"Wow!" said the rest of the kids.

Stuart fled back to his seat and buried his head in his arms. He kept it there for

the rest of the morning.

At recess, he hid behind an extra-fat pine tree.

At lunch, he pretended to be extremely busy counting his raisins.

On the bus ride home, he put his lunchbox on the seat beside him and stared out the window so no one would sit with him.

He would never make a friend now. Not after this morning. But so what? He had a really good friend in his old town, and look what happened. He had to move away.

Besides, the kids here looked like a lot of trouble. If he made friends with Olivia he'd just spend his whole life looking for her barrettes, or admiring her pocketbooks. If he made friends with Nacho he'd have to watch out for moldy food.

No, it was better this way. He had a maniac cat that he loved. He had met the trash collector yesterday, and they were going to be partners in saving junk. And he had his cape. All he had to do was be a little more careful about what he wished for from now on.

DAY TWO

A brilliant idea woke Stuart up at the crack of dawn. "Today I'm going to bring in something so interesting for Our Big Interesting World that all the kids will forget what happened yesterday," he told One-Tooth.

Stuart crept downstairs. Right away, he found a potato that looked just like his first grade piano teacher. He found an enormous hair ball that One-Tooth had spit up. These were wonderful things, of course, but most kids had seen potatoes and hair balls. To make up for what had happened yesterday, he would need something they had never seen before.

He raced outside and grabbed a shovel. He dug a nice, deep, round hole. It was an excellent hole, one of his best. But all that was in it was dirt. No gold, no jewels, no mysterious bones. No treasureful stuff at all.

Stuart dug another hole. Nothing but dirt. Again.

And again, and again, and again.

Plenty of holes. Plenty of dirt.

Plenty of nothing to bring in for Our Big
Interesting World.

Stuart dropped
his shovel. He was
getting worried.

Great things had been happening to him
since he had made his cape. He had
grown toast, he had flown, some animals had come over to play.

But lately, not-so-great things
had been happening. Yesterday,
his clothes had disappeared.

Stuuuvvaaaaaart

And now this. Maybe his cape wasn't working anymore. Maybe it was turning against him.

"Stuuuuu-aaaart! Time for breakfast!"

Aunt Bubbles's voice was very small, and Stuart could barely see his own house in the distance. He must have been digging for a long time.

He bent down to pick up his shovel. It was stuck. He tugged and pulled it free, but something was caught on the end.

It was a hole! A hole had peeled out of the ground and was dangling from his shovel! This had never happened before. But of course, he had never had a cape before.

The hole was beautiful and delicate, like a bubble with the top cut off. Carefully, Stuart lifted it from the shovel and blew the dirt off. He folded it up and put it into the pocket of his cape.

Inside, Stuart drank three tall glasses of orange juice. Digging was thirsty work. "I have a hole in my pocket," he told his family.

"A big one?" asked his mother.

"Yep," Stuart answered proudly. "Nice and round, too."

"Don't put any money in it," warned his father.

"I wasn't going to," Stuart said.

"I don't have time to sew it up today," said Aunt Bubbles.

"I don't want you to sew it up," Stuart explained. He smeared a glump of jam over his toast and shook his head. Grown-ups.

All through Our Big Interesting World, Stuart suffered in silent gloom. One girl took off her shoe and showed where a snake had almost bitten her. A boy with braces showed his collection of things that had gotten stuck in them. *These kids probably have hundreds of friends*, Stuart thought miserably.

If only he had more time, he probably could have found something amazing. By now, all the kids would be crawling all over themselves trying to be his friend. "Hey, Stuart," they'd say. "Show us that amazing thing you found again!" Stuff like that. Stuart laid his head on his desk to imagine what it would be like.

Just then, one of the big kids knocked on the door and handed Mrs. Spindles a note. Mrs. Spindles read the note. She gasped and clutched at her throat. Her eyes grew so large that Stuart wondered if they were going to pop out of her head and go zinging across the classroom. He would really like to see something like that.

"Attention, class!" Mrs. Spindles cried. "I have an emergency announcement!"

"Holes!" she read. "Hundreds and hundreds of holes! Neighborhoods have been finding them all morning. Detectives and scientists have been called in. Be on the alert today, and report anything unusual."

Mrs. Spindles dropped the note. "Oh, my dearest blue heavens!" she wailed. "Whatever could it be?"

HOLES!

"Hailstones, probably," Olivia said. "I'm going to have to wear a lot more barrettes."

"Giant earthworms," Nacho said. "We're going to need some really big robins to eat them!"

All the kids had lots of ideas for what could have made so many holes. Each idea made Stuart feel worse.

Finally he raised his hand. "Maybe it was a kid," he said in a voice that came out a little squeakier than he wanted. "Maybe a plain old regular kid was just digging around, looking for something."

"That is quite impossible, of course," Mrs. Spindles frowned. "Stuart, this is a very serious situation, and it is not the time for jokes."

Stuart's head hurt. This was turning into a rotten day. His arms were just about falling off from all the digging. He still hadn't found anything no one had ever seen before. The teacher thought he was making jokes.

And then he realized he had an even bigger problem: all that orange juice. He checked the clock — the bell wouldn't ring for hours. He'd never make it. He raised his hand. "I have to use the bathroom."

"It's at the end of the hall, next to the teachers' room," Mrs. Spindles told him.

Stuart wrote the directions down. They sounded simple, but he wasn't fooled. He knew simple things could get tricky fast. *I will not get lost; I will not get lost,* he repeated to himself all the way.

I will not
GET LOST...

TEACHERS'
ROOM

And he didn't. There at the end of the hall,
right next to the teachers' room was the boys'
bathroom. But of course getting lost was
only one of the things that could go wrong.
Getting stuck inside was another.

Stuart used the bathroom faster than
anyone had ever used it before in the
history of the world. He washed his
hands even faster. He was almost out

of there, but his heart began to squeeze
in fear. *I will not get stuck inside;
I will not get stuck inside*, he told his
worried mirror face.

By the time Stuart dried his hands, he
was a teeny bit panicked. He tore across
the room, skidded to the door, and yanked
the handle, *hard*.

Too hard.

Stuart stared at the door handle in his hand and tried not to cry. He didn't really care about being locked inside the boys' room. But pretty soon Mrs. Spindles would notice he was missing. She'd find out the

STUCK

door was stuck, and she'd call the firemen to get him out. It would probably be on the evening news. No one would ever want to be the friend of someone like him.

He was eight years old, and his life was ruined.

Stuart leaned his head against the wall and stroked his cape sadly. He had made the cape so interesting things would happen to him, but this was not what he had had in mind.

He wished he could just crawl into a hole and disappear.

And then it occurred to him: Maybe he could.

Very gently, Stuart pulled the hole from his pocket. He shook it out and spread it against the wall. A little tunnel appeared. It was too dark to see anything beyond, but he took a deep breath and squeezed himself through. Anywhere was better than the boys' bathroom.

Stuart poked his head out the other side of the tunnel.

The room beyond was loud and full of teachers. A bunch of them were watching cartoons on television. A few were reading comic books on the floor with their feet on the walls. Two of them were jumping on a couch, making faces at each other. Giant boxes of doughnuts were scattered all around, and everybody was chomping gum or puffing cigars like crazy. Signs all over the room read: NO KIDS ALLOWED!

Wow, thought Stuart, *so this is the teachers' room!* One teacher stuffed three doughnuts into his mouth all at once, then stuck out his tongue. The others laughed and clapped him on the back. A teacher next to him made a rude noise. The others laughed and clapped her on the back, too.

Just then the door opened and Mrs. Spindles ran in. Someone hit her with a spitball. Mrs. Spindles hurled a doughnut back. "I can't play," she said. "One of my students got locked in the boys' room."

Mrs. Spindles picked up a phone and dialed. "Hello, hello!" she cried. "Code 3 at Punbury Elementary! Send the firemen right away!" Then she ran out of the room.

Stuart gulped in horror. He had to get back to the classroom, right now — but how? He couldn't just walk through the door, or jump out a window. There was only one thing that might work. . . .

Before he could worry about everything that might go wrong, he dropped to the floor. He reached behind him and peeled off the hole. Then he crawled to the nearest wall, slapped the hole against it, and made his escape into the hall.

Back in room 3B, Mrs. Spindles was nowhere to be seen. Stuart knew this was his big chance to turn all his bad luck into good. He climbed onto her desk. "I have something to show for Our Big Interesting World!" he announced.

"Something you have never seen before!"

Stuart led the kids down the hall. One by one, he showed them the hole into the teachers' room. One by one they bent down and looked through it. He could hardly wait to see their reactions.

And then one by one, they stood up and stared at Stuart as though he were crazy.

Stuart bent down and looked into the teachers' room. It was dark and totally empty inside. Just the way he suddenly felt when he realized everyone had left him there alone.

Stuart walked back to 3B as slowly as a person could walk without actually standing still. At this rate, he hoped, the other kids might be in fourth grade by the time he got there. On the way, he passed an exit. He stopped to poke his head out the door, wishing he could just run away.

There in the parking lot were all the teachers. They were watching a crew of firemen putting away their ladders. The chief was talking to Mrs. Spindles.

"The darnedest thing. There was no one in the boys' room at all. But it's a good thing you called. We found two more of the Punbury Holes!"

Another fireman joined them. "Yep. One in the boys' room, one in the teachers' room.

Right through the walls! Whoever did this
is probably a dangerous criminal!"

Stuart ran outside. He didn't want someone else to be blamed for what he did.
"Wait," he cried. "I made the holes!"

Everyone turned to stare at Stuart. A
man stepped forward. "I am the principal,"

he said. "You have obviously just had a very bad shock. In fact, we all have, so we are going to dismiss school early today."

"But really, it's because of my cape . . ." Stuart tried again.

"The principal is right, Stuart," said Mrs. Spindles. "You'll feel much better tomorrow. You might as well go home now."

Stuart decided to walk so he wouldn't have to face the other kids on the bus. With every step, his cape seemed to grow heavier and heavier, until he could hardly drag himself along. He sat down to rest outside Stanley the Trash Collector's barn, and his cape hung around him like a frown.

"Hi, Stuart," said Stanley. "You look as sad as yesterday's trash."

Stuart told him about his day. "I think my cape isn't working anymore. I think it's making me unlucky. Maybe I should just throw it away."

"People throw stuff away too quickly,"

Stanley said. "You've got to give it a chance."

"I guess I could try wearing it one more day," Stuart sighed. "After all, things couldn't possibly get any worse."

DAY THREE

*T*here should be a rule, Stuart thought, that if you are late to school no one should talk about it. Being late is embarrassing enough.

"You are late this morning, Stuart," Mrs. Spindles said, as if anyone in the room hadn't noticed this.

"I'm sorry," Stuart said, feeling his ears begin to blow up. "I had to fill in about a hundred holes. I'm the one who dug them, not some dangerous criminal!"

"Oh, Stuart!" laughed Mrs. Spindles. "Stop pulling my leg!"

Stuart sank into his seat, stunned. *Why would she say that?* He wasn't even close enough to pull her leg. Plus, why would he want to?

He sighed. It was hopeless. Even though he was wearing all his clothes, and even though he had remembered not to drink anything this morning, he was *still* going to have a bad day.

Math was first. Today's lesson was the number twelve. Most of the kids already knew about twelve. They knew it was also called a dozen. They knew it was ten plus two. Or six plus six.

Stuart knew about twelve, too. So far so good. And then Mrs. Spindles said something so wonderful Stuart could hardly believe his ears.

"Now class," was the wonderful thing she said, "I want you each to draw a picture for twelve."

Finally! Here was his chance to make up for all the bad starts! He had been the best drawer in his old school. If another kid drew a mouse, people might think it was a zucchini squash or a hat. There was no way to tell. But if Stuart drew a mouse, everyone knew it was a mouse. Even grown-ups. That's how good he was.

He wanted to draw something really fabulous now. Something so good all the kids would fight with one another to see who could be the best friend of such a great artist. He took his special drawing pencil from the pocket of his cape and began.

Stuart worked so hard

he lost track of time. This happens to artists a lot. Pretty soon all the other kids were crowded around his desk to see what was taking so long. Here is what they saw:

Twelve students! There were twelve students in Mrs. Spindles's third-grade class. And every one of them was on Stuart's paper!

Stuart knew it was one of his best drawings. Very detailed. Still, his heart thudded with dread. Drawing people could be tricky. You never knew how people might react. They might get mad if you left off their ears or made their feet look a tiny bit like bananas.

"There's me!" shouted Olivia. "Stuart drew all my barrettes!"

"Awesome!" cried Nacho. "My feet look like bananas!"

All the kids were so happy to find themselves in Stuart's drawing.

"Let's show Mrs. Spindles," they said.

Stuart was secretly very proud. But he just said, "Well, okay. If you want to."

But where *was* Mrs. Spindles?

Olivia called down the hall. Nacho checked the playground.

"Just like your drawing," Nacho said. "Twelve kids and no teacher."

Stuart looked at his drawing. He looked at his pencil. He looked at his cape. *Of course.*

"Don't worry," he told the other kids calmly. As if losing a teacher were the most normal thing in the world. "Things like this happen to me all the time. I'll just have to *draw* Mrs. Spindles to bring her back. No problem."

But there was a problem: No room on the paper. The twelve students filled up the classroom. The swing set filled up the playground.

There was only one place left to put her.

"Help!" Mrs. Spindles's voice floated

down into the classroom. "I don't know what's gotten into me. I seem to have climbed up onto the roof!"

"Don't worry," Stuart called up to her. "I'll draw you a ladder."

But he couldn't do it! He couldn't draw a ladder, even though he had been the best drawer in his old school. *Too many straight lines.*

Stuart tried again. And again. And again.

He tried twelve times. Twelve ladders, each too crooked to use.

Stuart began to panic. Probably no kid in the history of third grade had ever put a teacher on the roof. He was going to jail for life, unless he could think up a *terrific* idea.

And then he did just that.

"Hold on!" he called up to Mrs. Spindles.

"You'll be on the ground in a few seconds." Stuart erased Mrs. Spindles's old legs and gave her some new, reach-the-ground ones.

Mrs. Spindles's new long legs waved wildly past the windows. The other kids dove for cover under their desks.

"Oh, dear!" cried Mrs. Spindles. "What in the world has happened? How will I tie my shoes?"

How will she walk around? wondered Stuart. *How will she fit in the classroom? And whatever made me think this was a good idea?*

"Hang on," he called, trying to sound cheerful. He got a big piece of paper. "I'm going to start all over."

Stuart bit his bottom lip to concentrate. Very carefully he drew Mrs. Spindles inside the classroom. With normal legs.

He drew twelve desks, and a flag, and a chalkboard. He drew Smiling Ed, the class turtle, and Sparky and Pal, the hamsters. It was the best drawing of his career. But it wasn't done.

Stuart grinned. Outside, where there was plenty of room, he drew twelve kids . . .

ALL PLAYING <u>TOGETHER</u>!!!

Stepping onto the bus going home, Stuart had the feeling something was missing.

It wasn't a bad something-was-missing feeling, like if you forgot to put your pants on. It was a good something-was-missing feeling, like if the poison ivy between your toes were finally gone.

He took a seat in front of Nacho and tried to think what it was.

Nacho tugged on his cape. "Will you draw *me* some longer legs?" he asked Stuart. "Like you did with Mrs. Spindles?"

Stuart studied Nacho. Nacho was short, like he was, but at least Stuart had a tall neck. Nacho was just plain short, all over. In fact, he was the only kid in third grade shorter than Stuart. This was too bad for Nacho, but very good for Stuart.

That's what was missing! Stuart wasn't *worried* anymore. He wasn't the shortest kid in the class. He hadn't thrown up from an egg salad smell, he hadn't forgotten everything he'd learned in second grade, and he hadn't gotten stuck in the bathroom.

At least not for very long. And even though he hadn't made any friends, the other kids had played with him.

It felt weird not having anything to worry about, but good. *Still*, Stuart would have drawn Nacho longer legs if he could have. Even though it would have made *him* the shortest kid in third grade.

"You can put sandwiches in your shoes

to make yourself taller," he told Nacho. "That's what I do sometimes. Ham and cheese is the best; tuna fish is not so good. But I can't draw you longer legs. My cape doesn't work that way. I only get one thing a day. One adventure."

"That's okay," Nacho said. "I can wait until tomorrow."

Stuart shook his head. "It doesn't work like that, either. It's a *different* thing every day."

Just then, Olivia stuck her legs across the aisle. "My legs are exactly the right length," she said. "But if I had longer hair I could wear more barrettes. So tomorrow you can draw me with longer hair, right down to my ankles. That would be a *different* thing."

Stuart sighed. It was hard to have to keep saying no. "I'm sorry. Every day the different thing that happens is a surprise to me. I never know what it will be, and I don't

get to choose." He turned his head to the window. Nacho and Olivia wouldn't want to talk to him anymore.

Nacho tugged on his cape again. "I get it. It's like the ties in your cape. Each one is different."

Stuart hadn't thought of this. Nacho was right. Olivia leaned over and whacked him with her pocketbook.

"I *like* surprises," she said. "Surprises are *presents*."

Olivia was right, too.

Olivia and Nacho stood up to leave at the bus stop before Stuart's.

"Tomorrow is Saturday," Nacho said.

"We'll come over early."

"Right," Olivia agreed. "So we don't miss anything."

When Stuart jumped off the bus, his cape streamed around him in a gigantic grin.

How to do a ~~terific~~ really good portrait of me (stuart)

by stuart

1. Begin with my head and shoulders

2. add my glasses and ears (not too big)

3. then put the nose (thin) and eyes (smart)

4. next my hair (that's the tricky part)

HAPPY

NOT HAPPY AT ALL!

hello!

5. Finally, add the mouth, cheeks, arms and eyebrows (very important). With these, you can make a lot of different expressions for your favorite HERO! Keep my portrait in your room (especially if you are a GIRL!).

NOTE: Don't forget to draw at least a dozen fingers!